Penny
AND HER SLED

KEVIN HENKES

GREENWILLOW BOOKS
An Imprint of HarperCollins*Publishers*

Watercolor paints and a black pen were used to prepare the full-color art.
The text type is 17-point Century Schoolbook.

Library of Congress Cataloging-in-Publication Data

Names: Henkes, Kevin, author, illustrator.
Title: Penny and her sled / Kevin Henkes.
Description: First edition. | New York, NY :
Greenwillow Books, an imprint of HarperCollinsPublishers, [2019] |
Summary: Penny has a new sled, but will it ever snow?
Identifiers: LCCN 2019007019| ISBN 9780062934536 (hardback) |
ISBN 9780062934543 (lib. bdg.)
Subjects: | CYAC: Sleds—Fiction. | Patience—Fiction. | Mice—Fiction. |
BISAC: JUVENILE FICTION / Readers / Beginner. | JUVENILE FICTION /
Imagination & Play. | JUVENILE FICTION / Animals /
Mice, Hamsters, Guinea Pigs, etc.
Classification: LCC PZ7.H389 Pel 2019 | DDC [E]—dc23
LC record available at https://lccn.loc.gov/2019007019

19 20 21 22 23 SCP 10 9 8 7 6 5 4 3 2 1

First Edition

 GREENWILLOW BOOKS

For Lois

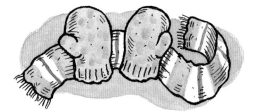

Chapter 1

It was winter,

but there was no snow yet.

Penny wanted snow.

She wanted to use her new sled.

Penny waited for snow

at the window in her bedroom.

She waited for snow

at the window in the living room.

"When will it snow?"

Penny asked Mama.

"Soon," said Mama.

But it did not snow.

Penny watched for snow

when she walked to school.

She watched for snow

when she walked home from school.

"Will it ever snow?"

Penny asked Papa.

"It will," said Papa.

But still it did not snow.

It seemed it would never snow.

"Do you want snow?"

Penny asked the babies.

The babies made baby noises.

"Me, too," said Penny.

"Do you want snow?"

Penny asked Rose.

Penny made Rose nod her head.

"Me, too," said Penny.

At night, Penny pretended
the stars were bright snowflakes
far, far away.
"It is snowing somewhere, Rose,"
said Penny.

One afternoon Penny wore

her scarf and sat on her sled

in the living room.

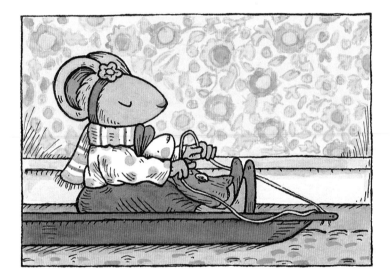

Maybe this will make it snow,

she thought.

It did not make it snow.

One night Penny wore

her mittens to bed.

Maybe this will make it snow,

she thought.

That night Penny dreamed

it was snowing.

The snowflakes in her dream

were as big and fat

as marshmallows.

Penny ate the snowflakes

with a fork.

When she woke up

there was no snow.

Penny hugged Rose.

"I do not think

it will ever snow," she said.

Chapter 2

Weeks passed.

It was cold.

The sky was gray.

The air was damp.

But there was no snow.

Penny could not go sledding.

But she did other things.

She went ice-skating

with Mama.

She went on walks

with Papa.

She drank a lot of hot cocoa.

Penny kept her sled

in the corner of her bedroom.

She thought her sled looked sad.

Another week passed.

And another.

And another.

Still there was no snow.

"I do not think it is going
to snow," said Penny.
"Maybe you are right,"
said Mama.
"There is always next year,"
said Papa.

"Next year is a long time
from now," said Penny.
She was quiet for a moment.

Then she said, "If there is no snow,
I will use my sled
for something else."

Chapter 3

Penny used her sled

to make a bridge

for her glass animals.

Then Penny used her sled

to make a house for the babies.

After that, Penny used her sled

to make a bed for Rose.

"My mitten is your pillow,"

Penny told Rose.

"My scarf is your blanket."

Rose napped all afternoon.

That night, Penny put Rose's bed
next to her own.
"Good night, Rose," said Penny.
"You are in your own grown-up bed."
Penny was lonely in her bed
without Rose.
Penny's bed felt too big
without Rose.

Penny got Rose and tucked her in

beside her.

"Sleep tight, Rose," said Penny.

"You will never sleep alone again."

The next day
Penny pretended her sled
was a magic carpet.
Penny pulled Rose
around the world.

"This is New York,"

    Penny told Rose.

"Now, we are in Japan,"

    said Penny.

"It is cold and snowy

    at the North Pole," said Penny.

"Button your coat."

Penny played
with her sled every day.
After a while,
she played with it less and less.

One day, Penny put her sled
back in the corner of her room.
She played with other things.

Chapter 4

The days were getting longer.

The days were getting warmer.

Penny still thought about snow

from time to time.

Penny said, "It was fun

to wait for snow

when I thought it would come.

But I do not want to wait

for it anymore."

"You could wait for something else,"

said Mama.

"What?" asked Penny.

"You could wait for spring,"

said Mama.

"Spring is too big a thing

to wait for," said Penny.

Mama was quiet for a moment.

"You could wait for something small

that is a part of spring,"

said Mama.

She smiled.

"You could wait

for a different kind of snow."

Penny knew only one kind of snow.

"What other kind of snow is there?"

asked Penny.

"Snowdrops," said Mama.

"You could wait for snowdrops.

They are the first flowers

to come up in the garden

every year."

Penny made a funny face.

"Snowdrops are not real snow,"
she said.

"No, they are not," said Mama.

"But snowdrops do not melt.

And they smell nice.

When they come up, you can pick

some and put them in your room."

Penny and Mama went outside.

They went to the garden.

Everything was brown.

"Nothing is growing," said Penny.

"Things are growing

under the ground," said Mama.

"The flowers are waiting

for spring, too."

Mama showed Penny

where the snowdrops would come up.

"What if the snowdrops

are like the snow?" said Penny.

"What if the snowdrops

do not come up this year?"

"They will," said Mama.

"That is what you said

about the snow," said Penny.

Mama was quiet

for a moment.

"I remember a few years
when it did not snow," Mama said.
"But I do not remember a year
without snowdrops."

Penny smiled.

"Good," she said.

"Then I will wait for snowdrops."

Chapter 5

Penny waited for the snowdrops.

She looked for them every day.

Penny looked for snowdrops

in the garden

before she went to school.

She looked for snowdrops

in the garden

after school.

"Remember, Rose, snowdrops

do not melt," said Penny.

"And they smell nice.

We can pick some

and put them in our room."

Soon, tiny green shoots
came up in the garden.
"Is that grass?" asked Penny.
"Those are snowdrops," said Mama.
"They will bloom soon."

More green shoots came up.

They grew a little bit

and a little bit more.

"The snowdrops
are almost ready,"
said Penny.

"Yes, they are,"
said Mama.

"Yes, they are,"
said Papa.

And then, one sunny day
when Penny came home from school,
snowdrops were blooming
in the garden.

Penny ran into the house

to tell Mama.

"Mama!" she said.

"The snowdrops are here!"

"Wonderful," said Mama. "Show me."

Penny led the way.

She stopped suddenly.

"Wait," she said.

"I have to get something."

Penny got Rose

and she got her sled.

Then Penny put on her mittens

and her scarf.

Mama was waiting.

She laughed when she saw Penny.

Penny pulled Rose

out to the garden.

"Rose, we finally have snow!"

said Penny.

Penny, Rose, and Mama
looked at the snowdrops
for a long time.
"They look like snowflakes,"
said Penny.
"Yes, they do," said Mama.
Then Penny picked one snowdrop
for herself, and one for Rose.

Penny took the snowdrops inside.

Mama put them in a little vase.

The snowdrops smelled nice.

And, best of all,

they did not melt.